Loud Lips Lucy

by

Tolya L. Thompson

Illustrated by

Juan R. Perez

Savor Publishing House

Dedicated to my mother, Laverne Morris Palmer,
and all those who had faith. TLT

Dedicated to my wife, Sandy, and my two daughters,
Kristen and Lauren. JRP

Loud Lips Lucy
Copyright © 2002 by Tolya L. Thompson
Illustrations by Juan R. Perez
Edited by Carol Anderson
Published by Savor Publishing House
Printed in Hong Kong by Palace Press International
All rights reserved
ISBN 0-9708296-0-4 Hardcover
Library of Congress Catalog Card Number: 2001-126013

Lucille Lucy was her name,
But Loud Lips Lucy is what they called her.
Now why on earth would they call her that?
'Cause boy could this little girl holler.

Lucy would open her mouth
So big and so wide,
I swear you could see
Every tooth inside.
And all those people
Who were anywhere near
Would have to stop
And plug their ears.

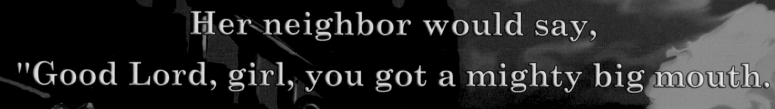

Her neighbor would say,
"Good Lord, girl, you got a mighty big mouth.

Would Ya?

Could Ya?

Please not shout?"

And Lucy would say,
in a loudmouthed way,
"Are you crazy?
Be quiet?
No how!
No way!"

Then off she went with her hands on her hips,
Saying,
"I'm all that plus a bag of chips."

Now Lucy shouted out this and that.
She loved to flap her lips and chat.
She would take a deep breath, fill her lungs with air,
And as loud as she could, she would scream,

"HEADS! LOOK OUT!
TIMBER!
WATCH YOUR STEP! BEWARE!
LOOK OUT, DON'T FALL!"

She'd scream these things for no reason at all.
But the one thing Lucy most loved to scream
Was "Yo, Mr. Ice Cream!"

Lucy's father warned her time and again,
"Baby girl, one day you'll lose your voice,
And that will be the end."

But Lucy was so proud of being rude and loud,
She couldn't heed his warning,
'Cause her head was in the clouds.

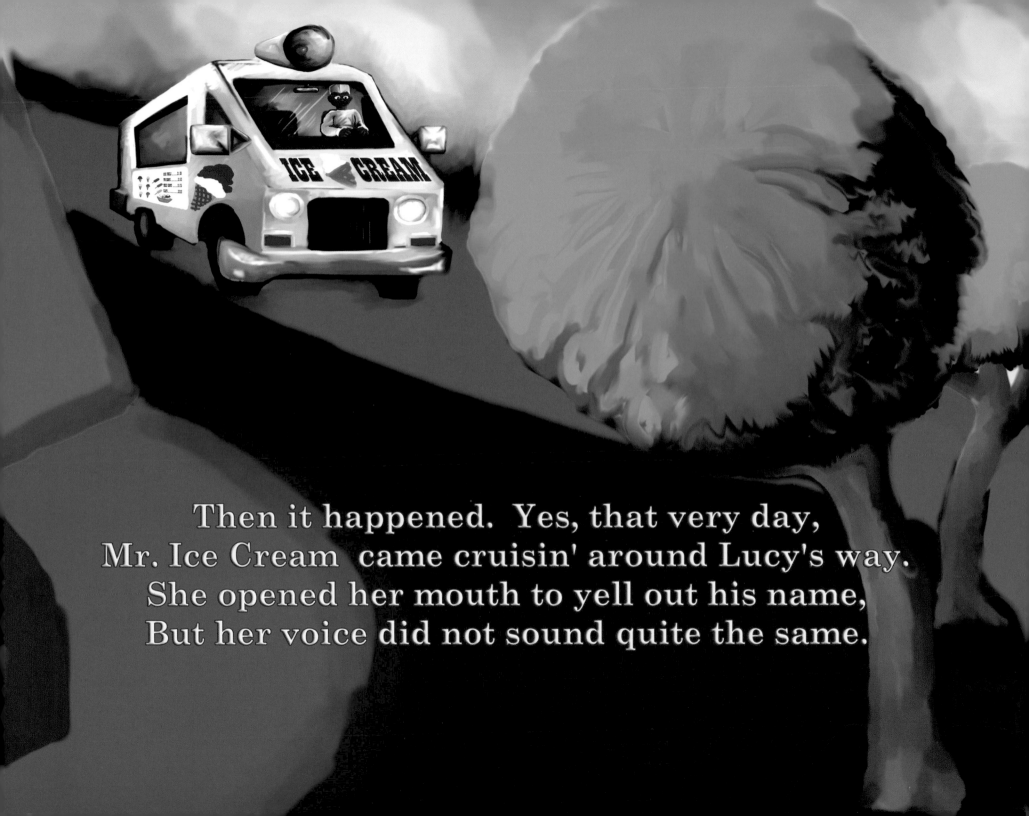

Then it happened. Yes, that very day,
Mr. Ice Cream came cruisin' around Lucy's way.
She opened her mouth to yell out his name,
But her voice did not sound quite the same.

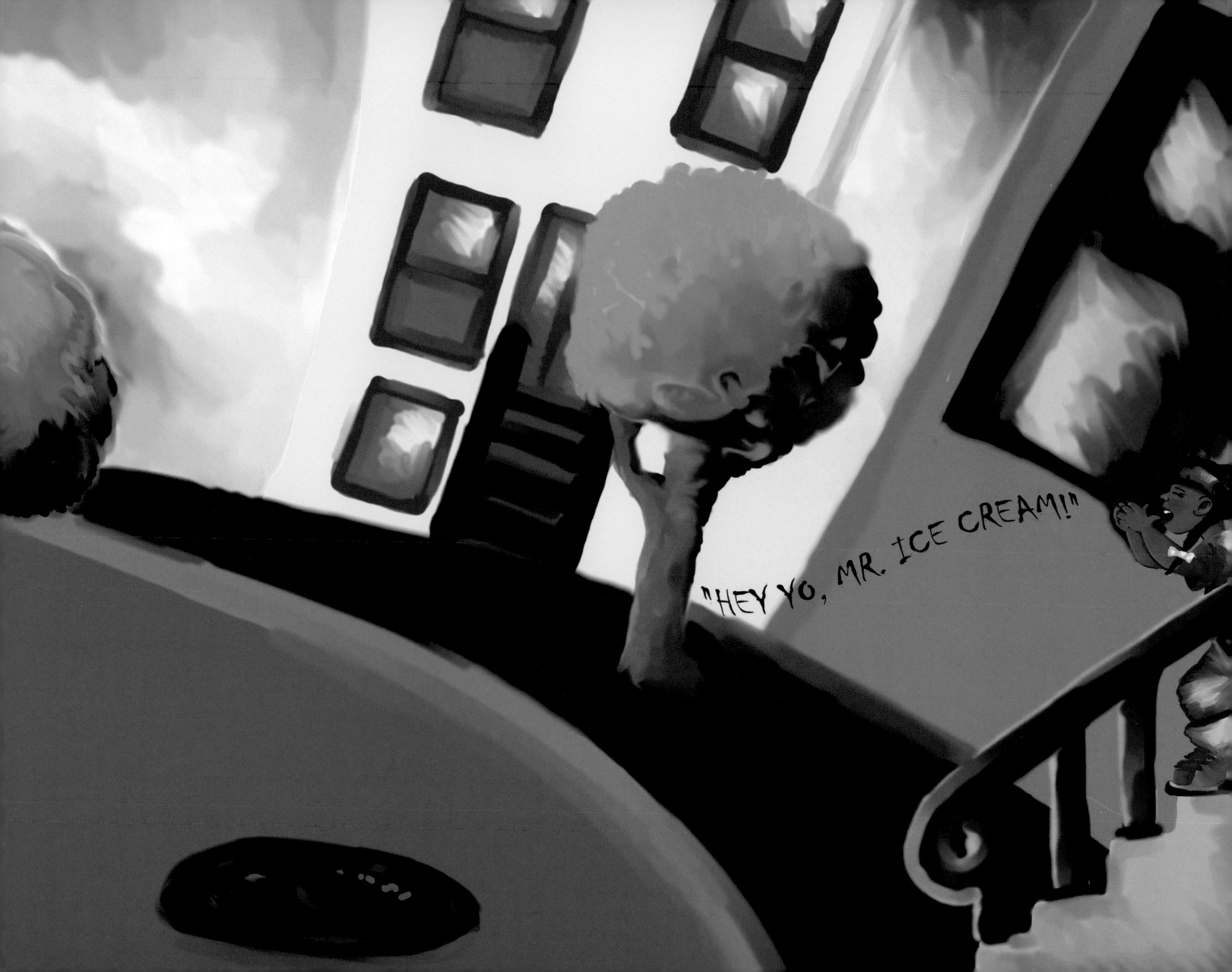
"HEY YO, MR. ICE CREAM!"

"Oh no," whispered Lucy.
"Something isn't right.
My throat is feeling scratchy
And it's feeling tight.
Let me clear my throat
And give it one last try.
I have to hurry,
The truck is passing me by."

So Lucy cleared her throat and yelled again.

"Oh no," she whispered.

"I've lost my voice. Believe it, it's true.

My life is over. I'm finished. I'm through!

I have to find it. I have no choice. What am I without my voice?

Now let me think.
Where could it be?
I didn't drop it down the sink.

Well, don't just sit there! Help me look!
I could have lost it in this book!
I'll search in the trees and you search on the ground.
My voice has to be somewhere around.

Or could it be between my toes?

I still don't see it anywhere. I bet I lost it inside my hair.
Lots of things get lost in there.

Would somebody tell me where my voice could be?
Maybe it ran away from me."

So poor Lucy began to pout.
She sat by the tree with her lips poked out.

Suddenly, she heard *tweet, tweet* coming from the tree. "That must be my voice calling for me," grumbled Lucy.

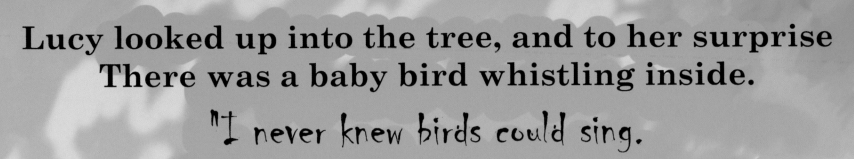

Lucy looked up into the tree, and to her surprise
There was a baby bird whistling inside.

"I never knew birds could sing.

That is the most incredible thing,"
Said Lucy.

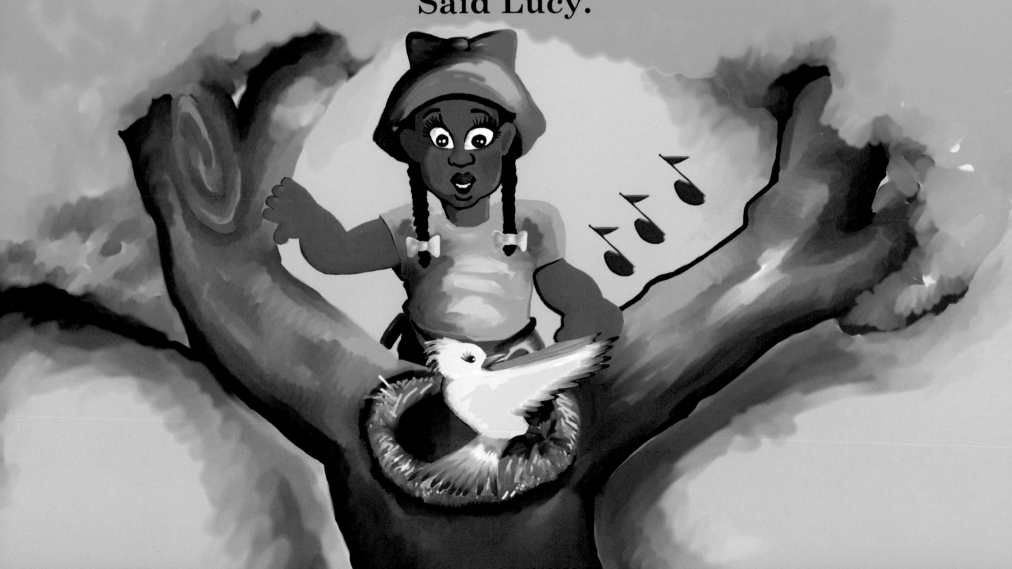

Then she heard chirping so loud and so clear.
"That must be my mama saying, 'Lucy girl, I'm over here,'"
thought Lucy.

But relaxing in the tree was the cricket that had chirped.
"I could have sworn that crickets burped,"
Thought Lucy.

¡Ay, Dios mio!

Shortly afterward, she heard, *"Whoooo, whoooo."*
"Who is that making that *whoooo?"* demanded Lucy.
"Wait, I know who is making that *whoooo.*
It's a cow. Yes, cows go *whoooo."*

But when Lucy looked high in the sky,
an owl going *"Whoooo"* was flying by.

As Lucy sat under the tree absorbing the sounds,
Some screaming children came strolling around.
"Shut your lips and park your hips,"
demanded Lucy. "I'm listening."

The children's mouths dropped to the floor.
They had never seen Lucy be quiet before.
So the kids all did what any kid would do.
They parked their hips and listened, too.

"Do you hear that?" asked Lucy.
"This world is filled with sounds galore,
And I want to hear more.
Yes, more!

Chirp

Whoooo

Tweet

Moooo

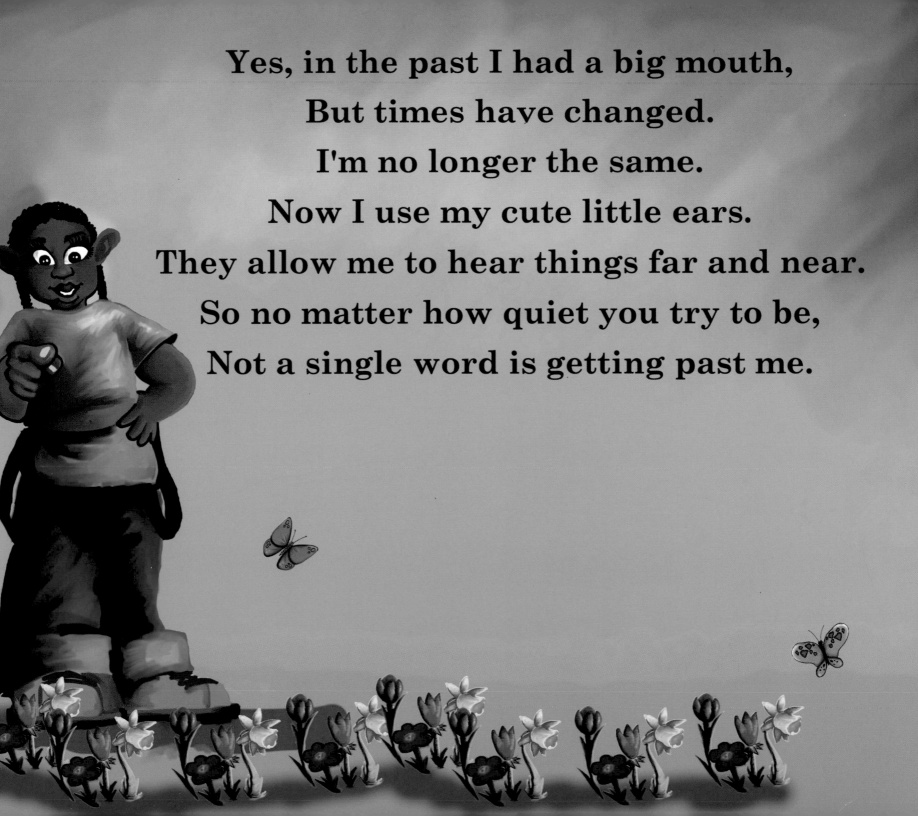

Yes, in the past I had a big mouth,
But times have changed.
I'm no longer the same.
Now I use my cute little ears.
They allow me to hear things far and near.
So no matter how quiet you try to be,
Not a single word is getting past me.

And look what's happened
Since I stopped yappin'.
My voice has decided to come back around.
Now I truly appreciate how wonderful I sound.
But I won't abuse it the way I did in the past.
I'll use it when I need it to make sure it lasts."

As the sun went down and the sky became dark,
Lucy gave advice to the children in the park.
"Don't holler and scream and act like a fool.
Use your ears, they're really cool.
And you'll be amazed at the things you find
when you close your mouth and open your mind."

Smartie

As I'm sure you know, our dear friend Lucy didn't really lose her voice. She simply developed a bad case of laryngitis. Laryngitis occurs when the larynx and the vocal cords, the two parts of your body that are responsible for producing sound, become red and swollen. There are several things that can cause the larynx and the vocal cords to become inflamed: viral and bacterial infections, harsh chemicals and gases, and simple overuse and abuse, as was the case with Lucy.

A person with laryngitis usually has a husky-sounding voice, but if the laryngitis is severe that person may have no voice at all. The treatment for laryngitis is simple: Stop talking and rest your voice. A warm, moist environment and steam inhalations have also proved to be very beneficial.